UGH

STORY BY

Arthur Yorinks

PICTURES BY

Richard Egielski

Michael di Capua Books

Farrar · Straus · Giroux

NEW YORK

For the people of Terre Noire

A.Y.

For Denise and Daisy

R.E.

Many, many, many, many, many years ago, there lived a boy. His name was Ugh. A good boy, Ugh lived with his two brothers and two sisters in a small cave by the sea.

Yes, life was simple. For fun, everyone went to the grove and watched dinosaurs eat trees. Everyone, that is, except Ugh.

His brothers and sisters made him stay behind and clean the

cave and find food and wash clothes. Ugh worked day and night, scrubbing, slaving.

No, for Ugh, life was miserable.

Still, he had hopes. In spare moments he made things. A belt. A bowl. A basket. Things.

"Ugh! Goof-off! Go work!" his sister said one day, catching Ugh at his hobby.

"But, but me like baskets," Ugh answered. "Me be famous boy one day. Me be—"

"You be dumbbell!" his sister shouted, and she made Ugh go and paint the cave walls.

Oh, Ugh. Woe was Ugh.

One afternoon, at the world meeting where everyone in the world met, Oy, the local scientist, showed off his latest work. It was called: *The Wheel.*

"Wheel stink!" Eh, the hunter, announced.

"Who needs wheel?" said Um, the spear maker.

"Wheel? Big deal," said Ah, the doctor.

The world was not impressed. But Ugh was mesmerized.

That night, while his brothers and sisters were asleep, Ugh snuck away. Under moonlight, out of tree limbs, a basket, and wheels, he made a thing. A bicycle.

Soon dawn dawned. So Ugh quickly hid the bicycle behind a bush and rushed home.

"Where Ugh been?" his brother scolded.
"Rub feet!" a sister insisted.
"Get grub!" the other brother ordered.
"*Mop floor!*" his second sister shrieked.

But Ugh had other plans. Thinking of his secret project, he said to himself, "Me show everybody! Me be big shot someday."

And the day soon came.

At the next world meeting, Ick, the dirt seller, asked the group, "So? What's new?"

People shrugged their shoulders.

"Okay, that's it, see you next week," Ick said, when out of the woods came Ugh, riding his bicycle.

"That's brilliant!" said Eh, the hunter. "I want one, I want one!"

"Hey, you, genius, stop!" said Ick. But Ugh couldn't stop. He hadn't made any brakes.

The crowd gave chase. Ugh, thinking the world was mad at him, jumped off his bicycle and ran away.

"Hey, what a thing!" said Ick, admiring the abandoned bicycle. "Whoever make this, he be king!"

The world agreed.

So they organized a search for the extraordinary bicycle maker. The bicycle was brought to each and every home and people were asked to ride it. Whoever could ride the thing would be made king of the world.

It looked hopeless.

But finally the world knocked at Ugh's door. Ugh's brothers and sisters shoved him aside.

"Me first, me make wheel thing!" one sister claimed. She tried to ride the bicycle and fell on her head.

"Me now! Me genius!" a brother yelled.

"Me next, me next," the others cried out.

Not one of them could ride the bicycle.

Ugh stepped forward.

"Me make bike, me ride," he said. He hopped on and easily rode around the block.

The world cheered.

Ugh was proclaimed king and given a brand-new home.
His brothers and sisters were so upset they threw themselves
into the ocean and were all eaten by a whale.

Ugh never had to scrub a floor again. Every day he would ride down from his palace cave and people would say, "Look, it's Ugh, the boy king. Long live Ugh!"

Ugh be big-shot boy the rest of his happy life.